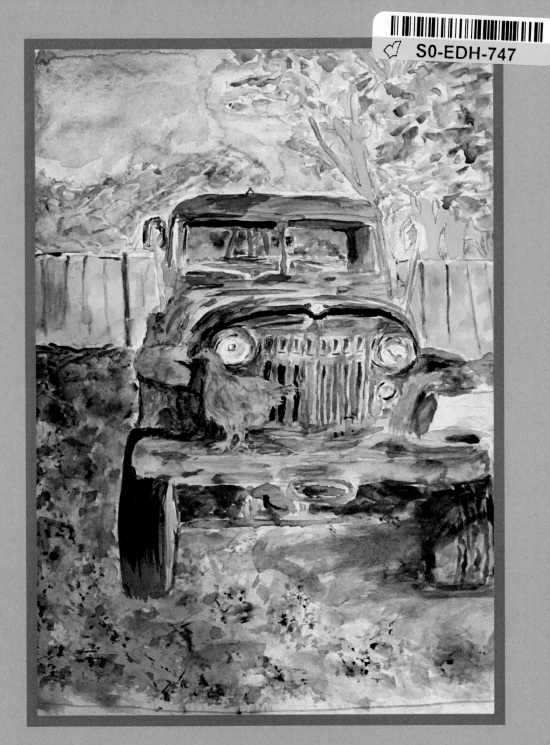

HORSIE WENT AWAY

Story And Pictures By Jani Mangan

This book is dedicated to my daughter Nicole and her children Ruger and Samson.

Copyright 2023

HORSIE WENT AWAY

Once upon a time, in a town in California, a trailer showed up to haul a horse away.

Oh Hello there, I'm Scittles. I'm a cat and I have a story to tell you. It's about the day Horsie went away.

It happened one sunny summer morning. I was up early and was just doing my morning stretches when I heard a motor running, loud cracking noises and lots of angry snorting sounds coming from across the street where a horse lives.

Jessie, a German Shepherd dog, who's been my friend since she was just a little pup, said "What's all that racket I hear? Climb a tree and see what you can see, Scittles."

Opi, Red and Barni came running out of their coop. They were just little chicks when they first arrived. They are big chickens now,… but… they still get easily frightened. "Scittles! Scittles! Scittles!" they cried, "We can't eat our breakfast, the bugs and worms are all running away, and that noise is scaring us."

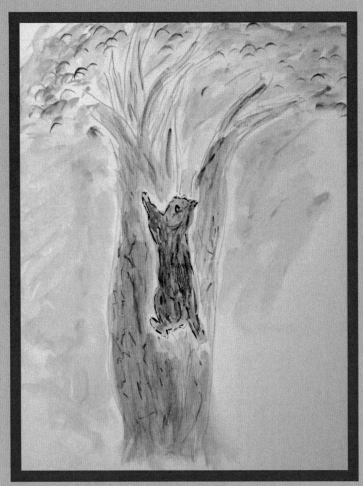

Zip zap zoom, I scurried quickly up a tree. I had a good view from way up there. The horse was breaking down the fence. A trailer ready to load up a horse was waiting.

"Oh what do you see way up there in the tree?" cried the chickens.

I called down to my friends telling them that it looked like the horse was going to be loaded into a trailer and taken away. I also told them that she was breaking a hole through the fence.

I said, "It seems to me that she is trying to get away."

"We can't let that happen! We must come up with a rescue plan to save her." Jessie declared.

"Scittles!!!", cried Opi, Red and Barni "We have to do something! What can we do to save that Horsie? This is terrible. We can't possibly let them take Horsie away."

"Jessie is right." I said, "We must come up with a rescue plan. It is up to us to save the horse. Think everyone! We must quickly come up with a plan!"

"I'm a herding dog! I can herd her through the broken fence and over to our yard! We have lots of room for a horse." said Jessie. "Opi, Red and Barni can be traffic guards while I cross the street to bring her over."

"We need a better plan than that." I said, "We are not allowed to bring new animals home without permission from our person, Steve. This is his property and he has rules, we would get in trouble for stealing the horse."

"I've got a better plan!" said Barni. "There is a bridge over the creek just a short way down the road. There is plenty of water for her to drink and the grass by the creek is ever so sweet. It will be a great hiding place. I can help Jessie herd her over there."

"No! Absolutely not, " I said to Barni, "Not a good plan! She can not spend her life in hiding. Plus it is cold, dark and damp under bridges. It may be a great place for trolls, but not for horses. Horses need sunshine and green fields to run and roll around on."

"This is ridiculous," said Red. "That horse just needs a good talking to about proper behavior. My goodness! I declare! She needs a timeout! Look at that destruction of property she's causing. That is no way to behave. No wonder she's about to get hauled off in a trailer. Imagine how much trouble we would get into if we went about breaking things and tearing down fences. She has got to learn to follow some simple rules. I'm going to go straight over there and straighten her out. I'll tell her to get up early, brush her teeth, make her bed and lay her egg before she goes out to play in the pasture. If she does that and NEVER breaks the fence or damages other property, there would be no need to have her hauled away."

"Umm Red," I said, "You do know that horses don't lay eggs, right?" "Oh fine then." Red said. "Cheese! If she just laid cheese before going out to play none of this would be happening".

"Red!" I said, "Cheese is made from milk...Cows make milk.....oh nevermind. That is NOT a good plan".

"Cows! Cows! Cows! That's it! I have the best, most wonderful plan of all time!" exclaimed Opi, as she jumped up and down. "I am the cleverest chicken of all. Who wants to hear my plan?".

"I do! I do! I do!" Everyone cried . We all looked at Opi, waiting to hear what her grand plan could be.

"Okay Opi, we are listening. Tell us what your plan is." I said.

"Well," said Opi, "you mentioned cows just now, and there happens to be a field full of cows right next door. The cows have a nice big green pasture that the horse can run around and roll about on. Jessie and I can take the horse there. I'll show horsie how to crouch down and fluff up her tail feathers to make her rump look bigger in the back. Then she just needs to keep her long neck low to the ground like she's grazing so she's lower in the front. I'll warn her not to raise her neck up so her mane won't show because her long neck and mane would be a big clue that she is a horse and not a cow. This is it! This will work!"

Opi crouched down saying, "See, look at me, I can show her just what to do to disguise herself as a cow. It is the most perfect idea in the whole wide world."

I had to tell Opi that I did not agree with her plan either. "The problem," I explained to Opi, "is that it never works trying to be something that you are not. It takes a whole lot of energy and effort, and in the end it never works anyway. It is a very sad thing not to be true to yourself and honest about things that are important to you, like running around with your head held high. That's what the horse truly loves to do. Plus, staying bent over like that will give her such a stiff neck... and Opi,... she is a horse and does not have any tail feathers to fluff up."

I was just about to think up a plan of my own when I heard a truck pull out of the driveway across the street. When I looked over, I saw the trailer with the horse on it headed down the street.

While we were busy arguing about a plan, the horse was loaded up and hauled away. All I could see was her tail as the trailer headed away down the road.

It was a very sad day...the day that Horsie went away. I carefully backed down the tree (I don't know why it is always so easy to go up, but so hard to get back down again).

We were all so sad. It was such a calamity that Horsie went away. We didn't know what to say to each other.

Jessie climbed the little hill and sat licking her paw for most of the day, while the chickens went their separate ways silently scratching at the ground.

I climbed up on a fence, facing the empty pasture. I didn't even go in for lunch. I sat on that fence all day long wondering about what may have happened to the horse. At some point I fell asleep but was suddenly startled awake by a rumbling of tires. "Guys, guys, look, do you see what I see?" I called out to my friends.

They came running up to me shouting "What? What? What?"
Jessie peeped through her peep hole, while Opi, Red and
Barni flew up to the top of the fence to see what I could see.

Horsie was back! Out of the trailer she pranced. She looked so happy and proud. A fancy hat was on her head and a ribbon with something written on it was around her neck. She was licking a pink fluffy cloud-like thing on a stick. We were so surprised to see her. Where had she been and what was that thing written on her ribbon, we all wondered.

"Aha!" said Jessie, "She must have gone to the doctors. Do you see that sticker on her ribbon? I got one just like that when I got my shots. It's an "E" for being an excellent patient. If you don't bite the doctor you get one of those. That explains it all!" exclaimed Jessie.

I must have had a better view than Jessie, because what I saw was a number and not a letter. "That looks more like the number "3" than the letter "E"." I said.

"I love the number "3", I just had a birthday card with the number "3" on it." cried Barni. "It must be her birthday! That explains why she has such a beautiful fancy hat on, it's a birthday hat. It's a "3" for her birthday."

"Barni, she was already a big horse when you were just a little baby chick, that makes her older than you." I explained.

"Well," said Red, "She must have started school,... and I say it's about time! She will certainly learn how to behave better and learn to follow rules at school. I hope we can count on her not breaking any more fences or causing any other reckless damage. It most certainly is a "3" for third grade."

"Red, School does not start with 3rd grade. 1st and 2nd grades are before 3rd grade. There is also kindergarten and preschool to be considered." I replied.

Opi started rolling around on the ground laughing. "Ha ha ha, I know what the number "3" is for." she said.

We were all pretty happy that Horsie was back. It had been a long sad day for all of us, so it was nice to see Opi happy and laughing.

"Alright, Opi", said Scittles, "share your guess with us. We're very curious to know what's so funny."

"It's a "3" for time." said Opi, "You see, it is now afternoon snack time. It's "3" for **3 O'Cluck'.** Ha ha ha get it? See look, **'it's 3 O'CLUCK'**, **'3 O'Cluck'.** Snack time, snack time for chickens and ducks!"

"Opi, that rhymes!" said Jessie, as she started to roll about laughing as well.

We all needed a good laugh after our long sad day. I have to say, I really did not think Opi had the right answer. Opi was right about one thing though. It was snack time. I hadn't had any lunch, and was feeling pretty hungry. We headed up to the house for snacks and *thought* that was the end of the day and the story:

Horsie went away....but just for the day.

As we headed to the house, our person, Steve, came out to meet us and said, "Hey, everyone. Surprise! I just got tickets to the fair."

"We're going right now!" he said. "We can get something to eat, check out the contests, ride some rides, and watch the fireworks."

Needless to say, we were very surprised!!!

The mystery was solved!!!

Horsie must have gone to the fair and won a 3rd place ribbon.

"Load 'em up!", said Steve.

Off to the fair we headed.

THE END.

Epilogue

The truck rambled on towards the fair with us all talking excitedly:

"I hope they have cake," said Jessie. "Maybe the horse won a prize from a cake eating contest."

"But did you see her hat? I've never seen a more beautiful hat than that. She surely won a prize for that hat." said Barni.

"Or jumping," said Opi. "She is so good at jumping. I've seen her run across the field and jump so high it looked like she could reach the sky."

"Of course, Opi!" declared Red, "Jumping! Like in an obstacle course! You may be onto something there! A horse obstacle course! They have those at the fair. That surely must be it."

"Bye Horsie, we're going away... but just for the day!" Jessie shouted, as we drove past her.

"Actually, it's for the afternoon and evening,... but nevermind." I said.

THE END (AGAIN)

"May I go to sleep now? That was one long story to tell and I'm pretty tired." yawned Scittles.

Jani Mangan graduated from the University of California at Berkeley with a degree in linguistics and later obtained a doctorate degree in audiology. She has since retired from her career as an audiologist and is currently pursuing hobbies that include writing, playing banjo, watercolor painting, gardening and photography. She lives with her husband Steve and pets: Scittles, Jessie, Opi, Red and Barni, in Scotts Valley, California.

Made in the USA
Monee, IL
25 March 2023